To Leo,
May all your Christmas
wishes come true!

Love...................................

Leo is ≥**excited**≤
Christmastime is here!

He says, "I wish for lots and lots of fluffy snow this year!"

Leo writes to Santa.
The letter takes him ages.

"Perhaps I've wished for way too much…"
(There are over 50 pages!)

Dear Santa,

Leo decorates the tree
with twinkly lights that glow.

Christmas
decorations

Look at Leo up on stage.
He's in the Christmas play.

He wished to make
his family proud and
have the greatest day!

The kitchen's very busy.
Leo can smell baking.

"I wish that I could eat that bowl of cake mix Dad is making."

Leo wakes at 5 a.m.
"It's Christmas Day!
Yippee!"

He runs downstairs
to find a pile of
presents beneath
the tree.

This jumper's really **itchy**.
He tries to grin and bear it,
but Leo really wishes that
he didn't have to wear it!

Leo dresses warmly.
His wish for snow came true!

He's off to build a snowman now.
Perhaps he can build two!

Leo's sledging down the hill. "I wish I could *speed* up!"

His wish comes true,
his sledge is *fast*
when powered by a pup!

It's after Christmas dinner,
and everyone is snoring.
Leo says to his best friend,
"I wish it was less **BORING!**"

Later, Mum asks Leo,
"Did your **BIGGEST** wish come true?"
"Oh yes," he smiles,
"that wish was being…"

" ...here with **all** of you!"

Do you wish for fun with friends,
or a family trip that never ends?
Whatever it is that you hold dear,
keep your Christmas wishes here!

I wish...

Written by J. D. Green
Illustrated by Julia Seal

Copyright © Hometown World Ltd 2018
Hometown World Ltd
1 Queen Street
Bath
BA1 1HE

www.hometownworld.co.uk

Follow us @hometownworldbooks

Put Me In The Story is a registered trademark of Sourcebooks, Inc.

ISBN 978-1-78553-973-2
All rights reserved
Printed in Italy
HTW_PO201806

put **me** in the **story**®

Bestselling books starring your child!
www.putmeinthestory.co.uk

SANTA STOP HERE!